The End

(Almost)

By Jim Benton

Scholastic Press • New York

For Griffin and Summer

Copyright © 2014 by Jim Benton

ISBN 978-0-545-67536-9

10 9 8 7 6 5 4 3 2 1   14 15 16 17 18

Printed in Malaysia   108
First edition, March 2014

The text type was set in ITC American Typewriter LT Medium.
The display type was designed by Jim Benton.
The art was created using Adobe Photoshop.
Book design by Victor Joseph Ochoa

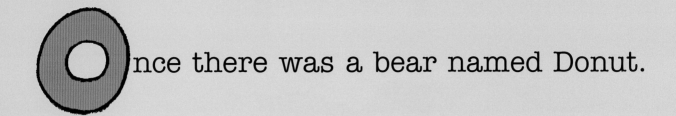 Once there was a bear named Donut.

That's me.

And he burped.

The end.

I said,
that's the end.

Yes.

The story is over.

Sorry, it's the end.
I mean it.
I'm sending you home.

Go home, Donut.

The end!!!
Go home, Donut.

Please don't forget
your shoe.

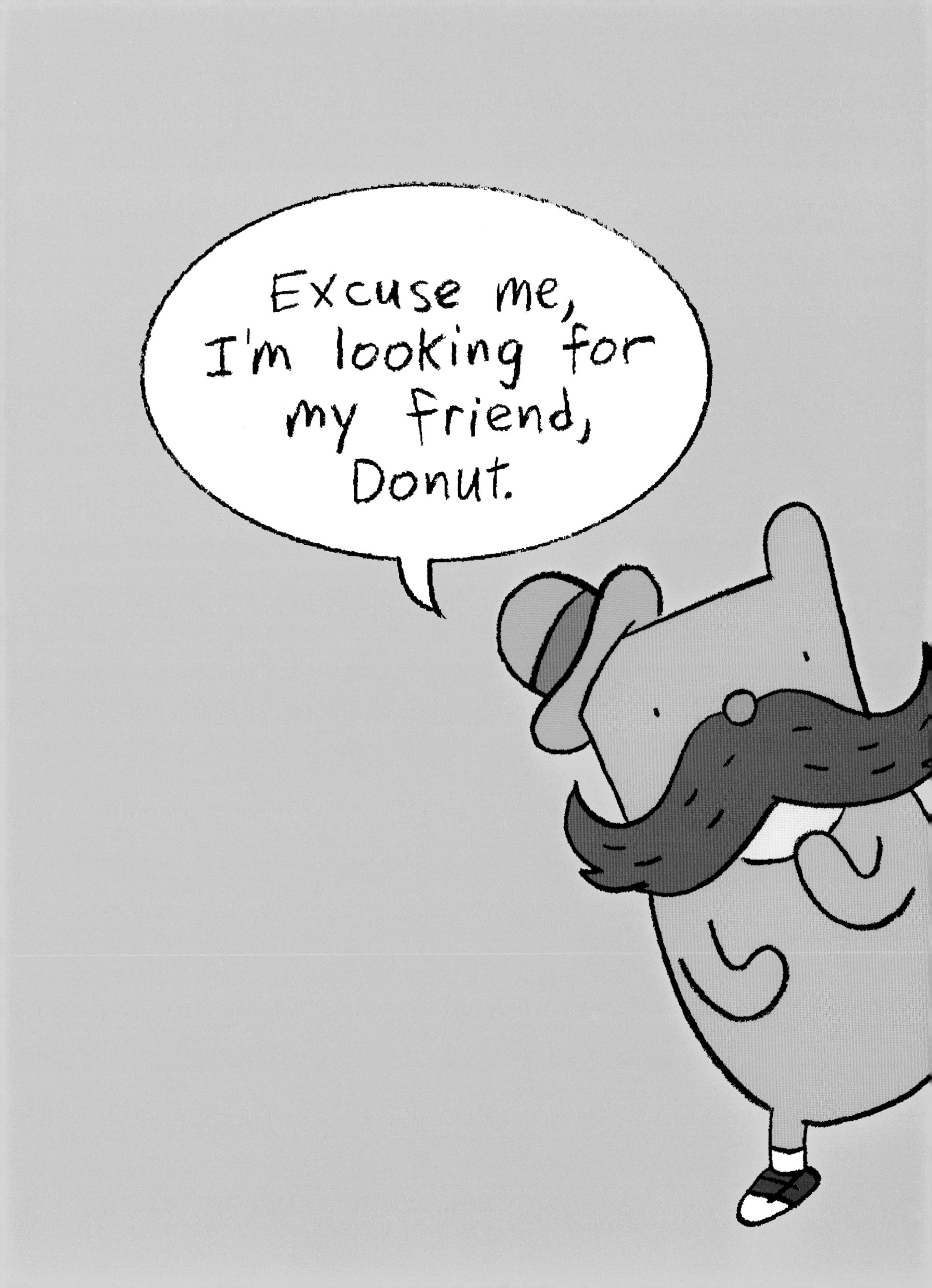
Excuse me, I'm looking for my friend, Donut.

Donut!
I know it's you!
It's time to go!

Donut is finally gone.

Yo

SNEAK

SNE

I see you, Donut!

What is it?

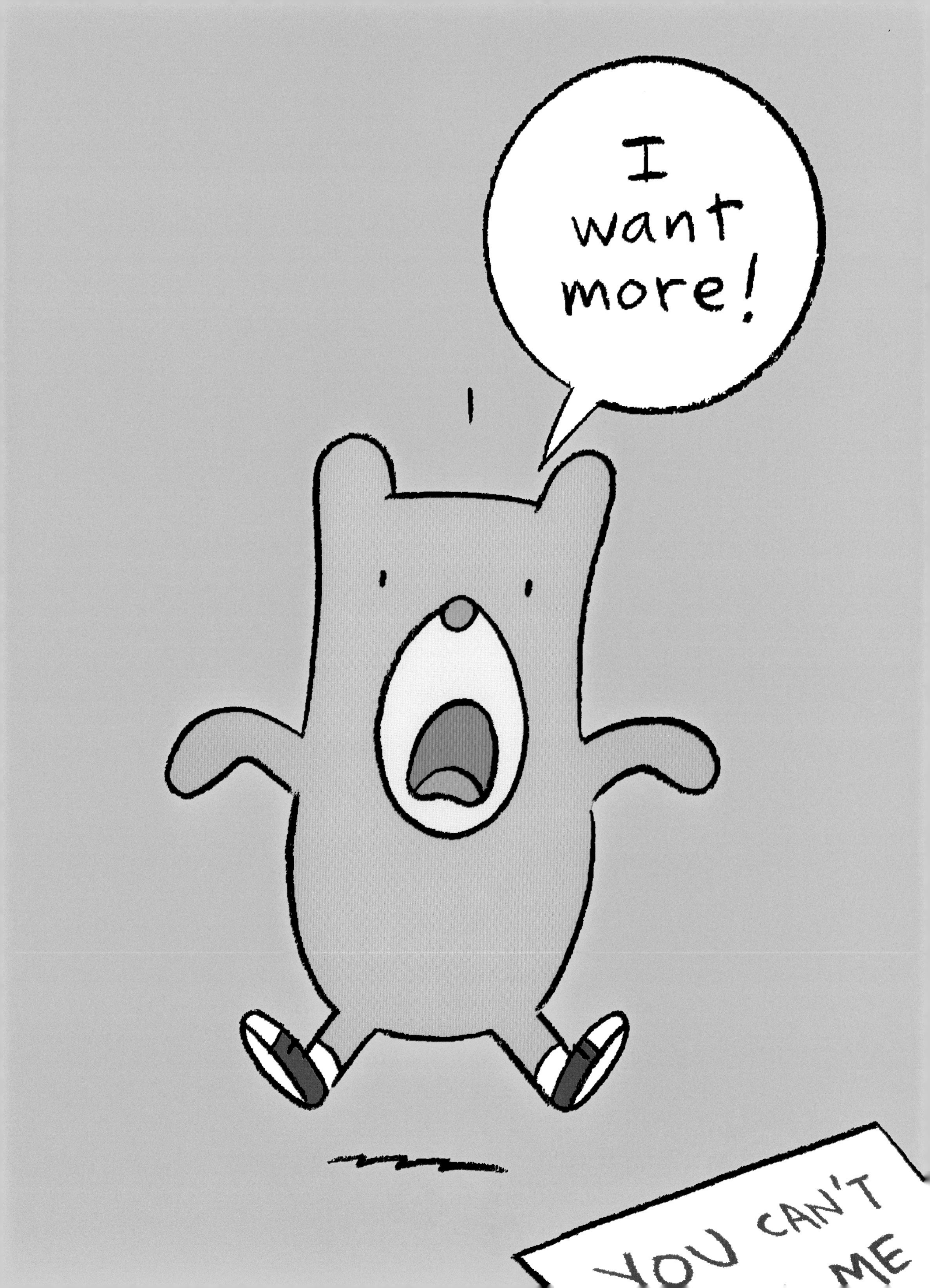
I want more!
YOU CAN'T
ME

Okay, okay!
Here's more:

Once upon a time, Donut,
his robot, and a
talking ice-cream cone
decided to go to the castle of
rainbow candy unicorns.
When they got there,
they discovered that . . .

Oops.
We're out of pages.
This time, it really is
the end.

Unless you want to read
it again . . .

The
End

(Really.)